A Break-of-Day Book

Ever since 1928, when Wanda Gág's classic *Millions of Cats* appeared, Coward-McCann has been publishing books of high quality for young readers. Among them are the easy-to-read stories known as Break-of-Day books. This series appears under the colophon shown above—a rooster crowing in the sunrise—which is adapted from one of Wanda Gág's illustrations for *Tales from Grimm.*

Though the language used in Break-of-Day books is deliberately kept as clear and as simple as possible, the stories are not written in a controlled vocabulary. And while chosen to be within the grasp of readers in the primary grades, their content is far-ranging and varied enough to captivate children who have just begun crossing the momentous threshold into the world of books.

Nate the Great

by Marjorie Weinman Sharmat
illustrated by Marc Simont

Coward-McCann, Inc.
New York

for Craig
the great

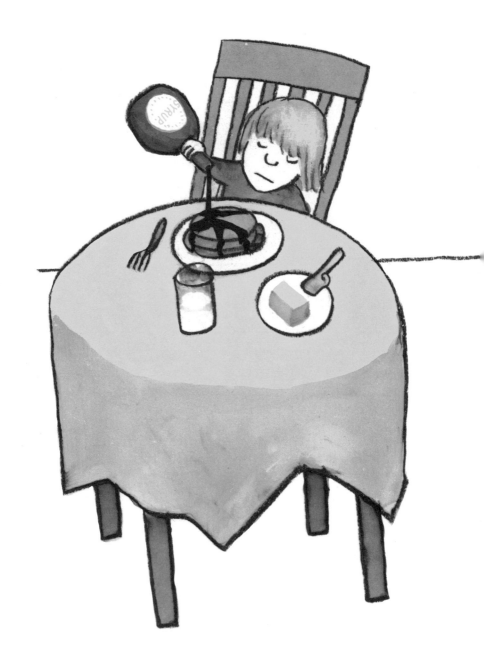

My name is Nate the Great.

I am a detective.

I work alone.

Let me tell you about my last case:

I had just eaten breakfast.

It was a good breakfast.

Pancakes, juice, pancakes, milk,
and pancakes.
I like pancakes.
The telephone rang.
I hoped it was a call to look for
lost diamonds or pearls
or a million dollars.
It was Annie.

Annie lives down the street.
I knew that Annie did not have
diamonds or pearls
or a million dollars
to lose.
"I lost a picture," she said.
"Can you help me find it?"
"Of course," I said.

"I have found lost balloons,
books, slippers, chickens.
Even a lost goldfish.
Now I, Nate the Great,
will find a lost picture."
"Oh, good," Annie said.

"When can you come over?"
"I will be over
in five minutes," I said.
"Stay right where you are.
Don't touch anything.
DON'T MOVE!"

"My foot itches," Annie said.

"Scratch it," I said.

I put on my detective suit.

I took my notebook and pencil.

I left a note for my mother.

I always leave a note

for my mother

when I am on a case.

Dear mother,
I will be back.
I am wearing my
rubbers.
Love,
Nate the Great

I went to Annie's house.
Annie has brown hair
and brown eyes.
And she smiles a lot.
I would like Annie
if I liked girls.

She was eating breakfast.

Pancakes.

"I like pancakes," I said.

It was a good breakfast.

"Tell me about your picture,"
I said.

"I painted a picture
of my dog, Fang," Annie said.
"I put it on my desk to dry.
Then it was gone.
It happened yesterday."

"You should have
called me yesterday,"
I said, "while the trail was hot.
I hate cool trails.
Now, where would a picture go?"
"I don't know," Annie said.
"That's why I called you.
Are you sure you're a detective?"
"Sure, I'm sure. I will find
the picture of Fang," I said.
"Tell me. Does this house have
any trapdoors
or secret passages?"
"No," Annie said.
"No trapdoors or secret passages?"
I said. "This will be

a very dull case."

"I have a door that squeaks,"
Annie said.

"Have it fixed," I said.

'Now show me your room."

We went to Annie's room.

It was big. It had yellow walls,

a yellow bed, a yellow chair,

and a yellow desk.
I, Nate the Great,
was sure of one thing.
Annie liked yellow.

I searched the room.
I looked on the desk.
And under the desk.
And in the desk.
No picture.

I looked on the bed.

And under the bed.

And in the bed.

The bed was comfortable.

I looked in the wastebasket.

I found a picture of a dog.

"Is this it?" I asked.

"No," Annie said.

"My picture of Fang is yellow."

"I should have known," I said.

"Now tell me. Who has seen
your picture?"
"My friend Rosamond has seen it,
and my brother Harry. And Fang.

But Fang doesn't count. He's a dog."
"Everybody and everything counts,"
I said. "I, Nate the Great, say
that everything counts.
Tell me about Fang.
Is he a big dog?"
"Very big," Annie said.
"Does he have big teeth?" I asked.
"Very big," Annie said.
"Does he bite people?"
"No," Annie said. "Will this
help the case?"
"No," I said. "But it might help me.
Show me Fang."
Annie took me out to the yard.
Fang was there.

He was big, all right.
And he had big teeth.
He showed them to me.
I showed him mine.
He sniffed me.
I sniffed him back.

And we were friends.

I watched Fang run.

I watched him eat.

I watched him bury a bone.

"Hmm," I said. "Watch Fang
bury that bone.

He buries very well.

He could bury other things.

Like a picture."

"Why would he bury

a picture?" Annie asked.

"Maybe he didn't like it,"

I said. "Maybe it wasn't

a good picture of him."

"I never thought of that,"

Annie said.

"I, Nate the Great,

think of everything.

Tell me. Does Fang ever

leave this yard?"

"Only on a leash," Annie said.

"I see," I said.

"Then the only place
he could bury the picture
is in the yard.
Come. We will dig in the yard."
Annie and I dug for two hours.
We found rocks, worms,
bones, and ants.
But no picture.

At last I stood up.
I, Nate the Great,
had something to say.
"I am hungry."
"Would you like
some more pancakes?" Annie asked.
I could tell that
Annie was a smart girl.
I hate to eat on the job.
But I must keep up my strength.
We sat in the kitchen.
Cold pancakes are almost as good
as hot pancakes.
"Now, on with the case," I said.
"Next we will talk
to your friend Rosamond."

Annie and I walked
to Rosamond's house.

Rosamond had black hair
and green eyes.
And cat hair all over her.
"I am Nate the Great," I said.
"I am a detective."
"A detective?" said Rosamond.
"A real, live detective?"

"Touch me," I said.

"Prove you are
a detective," said Rosamond.
"Find something.
Find my lost cat."

"I am on a case," I said.

"I am on a big case."

"My lost cat is big,"
Rosamond said.

"His name is Super Hex.
I have four cats.

They are all named Hex."
I could tell that
Rosamond was a strange girl.
"Here are my other cats," she said.
"Big Hex, Little Hex,
and Plain Hex."
The cats had black hair
and green eyes.
And long claws.
Very long claws.
We went into Rosamond's house.
I looked around.

There were pictures everywhere.

Pictures of cats.

Sitting cats. Standing cats.

Cats in color

and in black and white.

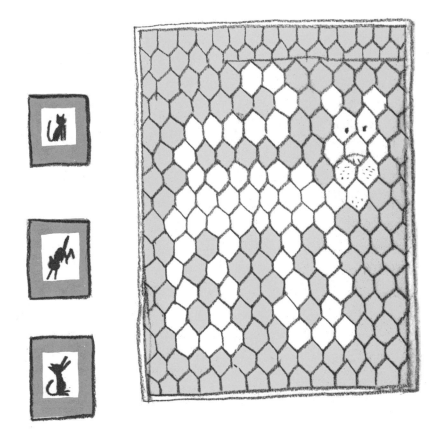

We sat down.

Little Hex jumped onto Annie's lap.

Plain Hex jumped

onto Rosamond's lap.

Big Hex jumped onto my lap.

I did not like Big Hex.

Big Hex did not like me.

"Time to go," I said.

"We just got here," Annie said.

She liked Little Hex.

"Time to go," I said again.

I stood up.

I tripped over something.

It was long and black.

It was a cat's tail.

"MEOW!"

"Super Hex!" Rosamond cried.

"You found him!
You are a detective."
"Of course," I said.
"He was under my chair.
Except for his tail."

Annie and I left.

It was a hard thing to do.

I could smell pancakes

in Rosamond's kitchen.

"Rosamond did not take
the picture of your dog," I said.
"Rosamond only likes cats.
And pancakes.
Now where is
your brother Harry?"

I met Annie's brother.

He was small.

He was covered with red paint.

"Me paint," he said.

"Me paint you."

"Good," I said. "No one has ever

painted a picture of me,
Nate the Great."
Harry took his paintbrush.
It was covered with red paint.
All at once I was covered
with red paint.

"He painted you," Annie said.

"He painted you."

Then she laughed.

I, Nate the Great, did not laugh.

I was on a case.

I had a job to do.

I looked around the room.

Harry had painted a clown,
a house, a tree, and a monster
with three heads.
He had also painted

part of the wall,

one slipper,

and a doorknob.

"He does very good work," I said.

"But where is my picture?"
Annie asked.
"That is a good question," I said.
"All I need is a good answer."
Where was the picture of Fang?
I could not find it.
Fang did not have it.
Rosamond did not have it.

Harry did not have it.

Or did he?

All at once I knew

I had found the lost picture.

I said, "I, Nate the Great,

have found your picture."

"You have?" Annie said. "Where?"

"Look!" I said. "Harry has a picture
of a clown, a house, a tree,
and a monster with three heads."
"So what?" Annie said.
"Look again," I said.

"The picture of the clown is red.
The picture of the house is red.
The picture of the tree is red.
But the picture of the monster
is orange."

"So what?" Annie said again.

"Orange is great for a monster."

"But Harry paints with red,"

I said.

"Everything is red but the monster.

I, Nate the Great,

will tell you why.

Harry painted a red monster

over the yellow picture of your dog.

The yellow paint was still wet.

It mixed with the red paint.

Yellow and red make orange.

That is why the monster is orange."

Annie opened her mouth.

She did not say a word.

Then she closed her mouth.

I said, "See!

The monster has three heads.

Two of the heads were

your dog's ears.

The third head was the tail.

Yes, he *does* do good work."

Annie was very mad at her brother.

I was mad, too.

I, Nate the Great,

had never been red before.

"The case is solved," I said.

"I must go."

"I don't know how

to thank you," Annie said.

"I do," I said.

"Are there any pancakes left?"

I hate to eat on the job.

But the job was over.

We sat in Annie's kitchen.

Annie and I. And Harry.

Annie said, "I will paint

a new picture.

Will you come back to see it?"
"If Harry doesn't see it first,"
I said.
Annie smiled. Harry smiled.
They even smiled at each other.
I smiled, too.

I, Nate the Great,
like happy endings.
It was time to leave.
I said good-bye to Annie
and Harry and Fang.
I started to walk home.
Rain started to fall.
I was glad I was wearing
my rubbers.

About the Author

Marjorie Weinman Sharmat began writing when she was eight years old. She started *The Snooper's Gazette* with a friend, and they supplied the paper with news from their own detective agency. Mrs. Sharmat, who has written many books for children, combines her love of mysteries and writing in NATE THE GREAT. She makes her home in Tucson, Arizona, with her husband Mitchell.

About the Artist

Marc Simont was born in Paris, but spent his early childhood in Barcelona. He studied art in Paris and New York and has been a muralist for various buildings, among them the Library of Congress in Washington. Mr. Simont won the Caldecott Medal for his pictures in *A Tree is Nice* by Janice May Udry. He has illustrated many books for children. He lives in West Cornwall, Connecticut.